This book belongs to:

_____

HAPPY PASSOVER, ROSIE

ROSIE

· STORY AND PICTURES BY ·

JANE BRESKIN ZALBEN

HENRY HOLT AND COMPANY | *New York*

Library of Congress Cataloging-in-Publication Data
Zalben, Jane Breskin. / Happy Passover, Rosie
Summary: A young bear named Rosie celebrates Passover with her family.
[1. Passover—Fiction. 2. Seder—Fiction. 3. Bears—Fiction.] I. Title.
PZ7 Z254Hap 1990 [E]—dc20 89-19979
ISBN 0-8050-1221-4

Henry Holt books are available at special discounts
for bulk purchases for sales promotions, premiums,
fund-raising, or educational use. Special editions
or book excerpts can also be created to specification.
For details contact:
Special Sales Director
Henry Holt and Company, Inc.
115 West 18th Street
New York, New York 10011

First Edition
Designed by Jane Breskin Zalben
Printed in the United States of America
1 3 5 7 9 10 8 6 4 2

In memory of my father, my uncle, Mama and Papa
—and that first Seder I remember, when I was three

The night before the first Passover Seder, Rosie and her brother Max hunted for stray bread crumbs with wooden spoons. Grandma dusted the shelves with a feather while Grandpa held a glowing candle and a small box for the crumbs.

The next morning birds were chirping when Rosie opened her eyes. The air felt like spring. Rosie and Max helped Grandpa burn the box of *chametz* while Grandma stirred the soup she was making for the Seder meal. She sighed, "Mmm. These matzoh balls are light and fluffy." Max whispered, "Remember last year when Papa made them and they were like bowling balls?" Rosie giggled, watching them float.

Before sundown family and friends arrived.
Aunt Gertie gave Rosie a huge wet kiss on
the cheek, and Uncle Hymie nearly crushed
her with his big hug.

When it was time for the Seder, Rosie sat
next to her cousin Beni. Grandpa picked up
the three matzohs in the blue-velvet pouch
embroidered with gold thread. He broke
the middle matzoh, the *afikoman*, in half
and wrapped it in a cloth. When no one was
looking, he hid the matzoh. Rosie wondered,
Where? And when? She thought she had been
watching Grandpa the whole time.

Then it was time to ask the Four Questions.
Rosie was the youngest, so she was supposed to
ask them all by herself. She had been practicing
with Max for weeks. Rosie looked at the faces

around the table. Mama smiled as Rosie began. "Why is this night different from all other nights? On all other nights we eat bread or matzoh: Why tonight only matzoh?" Papa smiled also.

Max helped a little with the second question.
Sara whispered the next one when Rosie forgot
a word. Rosie and Beni said the last question
together. Mama and Papa were very, very proud.
Everyone said the Ten Plagues and sang "Dayenu."

While Grandpa recited the Haggadah, Rosie spent most of her time under the table, crawling between her aunts' and uncles' legs. She peeked out when it was time for the bitter herbs, the *ḥaroset*, and finally the meal.

The family was so stuffed, nobody could move
an inch—except Rosie and Max and their cousins,
who ran around searching for the hidden matzoh.
Rosie looked under the pillow on Grandpa's chair.
"I found the *afikoman!*" she cried. Grandpa took

Rosie aside and gave her a shiny silver coin.
And he winked. Rosie gave Grandpa a big smile.
Then he poured a glass of wine for the prophet
Elijah and left it in front of an empty chair.
Rosie and Max played with Beni and Sara.

Suddenly there was a loud knock at the front door. Grandma opened it. Outside was very dark. "Is it the ghost of Elijah?" asked Uncle Hymie. Rosie trembled. Uncle Hymie began to chuckle. Then Aunt Gertie. Then Mama and Papa, and all the cousins. From beneath a coat came Grandpa. The relatives laughed. Very hard. Rosie didn't laugh at all. She wouldn't go near Grandpa for a long time.

Grandpa came over to Rosie when he saw she was
feeling better. "Sweetheart, I'm sorry I scared
you. See, it's me, Grandpa. I'll always be your
Zaide. Forever." And he touched his hand to Rosie's.
"Can I give you your special gift now?" Rosie nodded.

Grandpa gave her a kiss. A hug. And her own Haggadah.
Rosie hugged her Grandpa. "Happy Passover, Rosie."
"Happy Passover, Grandpa." Grandma came over
and hugged Rosie also. "And Grandma too."
Her apron still smelled of chicken soup.

THE SEDER PLATE

1. Egg (*beitzah*): A roasted egg symbolizes the festival offering in the Temple and the mourning of the destruction of the Temple. But the egg can also be thought of as a symbol of fertility and renewal.

2. Shank bone (*zeroa*): A scorched portion of the leg bone of a lamb represents the paschal offering, in memory of the ancient Temple sacrifice.

3. Bitter herb (*maror*): Sometimes romaine lettuce, sometimes horse-radish, this recalls the bitterness of slavery in Egypt.

4. Grated horseradish (*ḥazeret*): This additional bitter herb is eaten with the *ḥaroset* in a matzoh sandwich (*korekh*), to show life has two sides—the bitter and the sweet.

5. *Ḥaroset*: This sweet paste of chopped apples, nuts, and cinnamon mixed with a little wine represents the mortar used by the Israelites while they labored in bondage to the Pharaohs. *Ḥaroset* tempers the bitterness of the *maror*. A strip of cinnamon bark may be placed near the *ḥaroset* to represent the strawless clay bricks that the Israelites were forced to make in Egypt.

6. Parsley (*karpas*): A sprig of parsley represents spring, life, and hope. Dipped in salt water, the *karpas* suggests the bitterness of salty tears.

7. Matzoh: Three matzohs placed in the center of the Seder plate stand for the unity of the three tribes: Cohen, Levi, and Israel. (The matzohs may be put on a separate plate.) The matzoh itself is unleavened bread. It stands for the bread that was baking and didn't have time to rise when the Jews made their Exodus from Egypt.

THE FOUR QUESTIONS

The youngest child present asks:

Why is this night different from all other nights?

On all other nights we eat bread or matzoh:
Why tonight only matzoh?

On all other nights we eat any kind of herb:
Why tonight only bitter herbs?

On all other nights we don't dip the herbs even once:
Why tonight do we dip twice?

On all other nights we eat either sitting or reclining:
Why tonight do we all recline?

מַה נִּשְׁתַּנָּה הַלַּיְלָה הַזֶּה מִכָּל־הַלֵּילוֹת.

1 שֶׁבְּכָל־הַלֵּילוֹת אָנוּ אוֹכְלִין חָמֵץ וּמַצָּה. הַלַּיְלָה הַזֶּה כֻּלּוֹ מַצָּה:

2 שֶׁבְּכָל־הַלֵּילוֹת אָנוּ אוֹכְלִין שְׁאָר יְרָקוֹת. הַלַּיְלָה הַזֶּה מָרוֹר:

3 שֶׁבְּכָל־הַלֵּילוֹת אֵין אָנוּ מַטְבִּילִין אֲפִלוּ פַּעַם אֶחָת. הַלַּיְלָה הַזֶּה שְׁתֵּי פְעָמִים:

4 שֶׁבְּכָל־הַלֵּילוֹת אָנוּ אוֹכְלִין בֵּין יוֹשְׁבִין וּבֵין מְסֻבִּין. הַלַּיְלָה הַזֶּה כֻּלָּנוּ מְסֻבִּין:

E   ZALBEN, JANE BRESKIN
ZAL   HAPPY PASSOVER, ROSIE